Noth Happens on the Farm

by Kristi McGee
illustrated by Marsha Winborn

Harcourt
SCHOOL PUBLISHERS

Requests for permission to make copies of any part of the work should be addressed to School Permissions and Copyrights, Harcourt, Inc., 6277 Sea Harbor Drive, Orlando, Florida 32887–6777. Fax: 407-345-2418.

HARCOURT and the Harcourt Logo are trademarks of Harcourt, Inc., registered in the United States of America and/or other jurisdictions.

Printed in Mexico

ISBN 10: 0-15-351036-6
ISBN 13: 978-0-15-351036-6

Ordering Options
ISBN 10: 0-15-350602-4 (Grade 5 On-Level Collection)
ISBN 13: 978-0-15-350602-4 (Grade 5 On-Level Collection)
ISBN 10: 0-15-357961-7 (package of 5)
ISBN 13: 978-0-15-357961-5 (package of 5)

2 3 4 5 6 7 8 9 10   126   12 11 10 09 08 07

One day, Mom and Dad announced that we were moving to the country to get some peace and quiet. They needed a hiatus from the crazy city. With their jobs, they could both work from home, so it didn't really matter where we lived. It didn't matter to them, that is. The idea of moving to the country was completely unimaginable to me! It still is, now that we are here. Nothing ever happens here in the country.

I liked city life much better than this so-called peace and quiet. Back in the city, something was always happening. There were kids my age to play with. In the country, there is no one. I just had my eleventh birthday, and my parents were the only ones at my birthday party, unless you count the goat. He tried to steal some of my birthday cake right off the picnic table. We haven't really met anyone else, as in people, here yet.

After the cake, my mom and dad said they had a big surprise for me. Kwan, my best friend from New York, was coming to visit for a week! Back in New York Kwan and I were constantly together. We went to school together and played on the same basketball team. We liked the same foods and lived in the same apartment building. There was nothing precarious about our friendship. It was as solid as a rock.

Anyhow, I have to get ready for Kwan's visit. It's really fantastic that my parents are letting him come for a visit. They know I'm extremely bored here.

Mom keeps saying, "Emilio, why don't you go outside and enjoy the sunshine?" or "Emilio, come help me feed the goat," or "Emilio, your brain is going to rot sitting in this house reading comic books every day!"

What else is there to do? Outside there is just grass. Who would want to spend time out there in all that peace and quiet? I longed for honking horns and loud buses. What was I supposed to do here? Talk to the goat?

Finally, Kwan arrived today, and I was really excited. He's never been to a farm. I told him not to get his hopes up because it's extremely boring here. I could tell he didn't believe me. He took a train from the city to the closest stop to our house. It is about an hour away. Dad and I went to pick him up and found him saying good-bye to the train conductor who had been keeping an eye on him.

"Hey, Emilio!" Kwan yelled from the train platform.

"Hey, yourself!" I yelled back. Dad smiled to see a look of happiness on my face. It had been quite a while since that had happened. I know he feels terrible that I don't feel comfortable here in the country.

"I can't believe this place!" Kwan immediately said. "The train ride was great. I've never seen so many trees and such a beautiful river. I also saw birds I've never seen in the city!" Kwan was definitely more interested in these surroundings than I was.

"Did you bring any new comic books?" I asked eagerly. I couldn't wait to see all the new issues he had brought from the city.

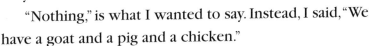

"Just one that I read on the train. Mom said I wouldn't need them here," reported Kwan. "She said there'd be loads of things to explore outside. What do you have on your farm?"

"Nothing," is what I wanted to say. Instead, I said, "We have a goat and a pig and a chicken."

"Cool! Where do they live? In a barn?" Kwan asked.

"That's right," I answered, "in a run-down old barn. It's kind of gross in there."

"I'll bet there are great hiding places. Is there a hayloft?" asked Kwan excitedly.

I started wondering if Kwan really had never been to a farm. He seemed to know so much about them. I didn't want to disappoint him, so I played along. "We'll check it out when we get home."

On the ride home, Kwan could hardly contain his excitement. He saw a wild turkey alongside the road, a groundhog chewing some grass, and a hawk circling above the woods. He pointed out all the horses and cows in the fields we drove by. There was a foal, or baby horse, with its mother. That seemed to be Kwan's favorite. Next was a ten-minute commentary on how big and beautifully blue the sky was. He couldn't believe the mountains and the valleys. They were fantastic in Kwan's eyes.

When we turned onto the dirt road that led to our farm, I thought Kwan was going to die of excitement. He had never been on a dirt road. The birds were singing, and some geese flew overhead. Kwan did not miss one thing! I could see my dad smiling. I knew he hoped some of Kwan's enthusiasm would rub off on me.

There's no need to tell you how much Kwan loved the old farmhouse. He thought my attic room, which was huge, I must admit, was the best thing he had ever seen. He loved the slanted ceilings and the old wood floors. He helped me build a fort using an old couch against the slanted wall. We decided we would go on an expedition the next day. Mom said we had better get to bed early. We needed to be well-rested for our hike.

9

The next morning, we went to the barn and got eggs from Greta's nest. She is our only chicken. Kwan was enthralled. "Talk about fresh!" he said. Eggs for breakfast was certainly not extravagant. However, from Kwan's reaction, you would have thought that Mom was serving us a gourmet meal.

After that, we prepared for a hike through the pastures and woods around the farm. We packed our lunches and embarked on our journey. Mom said, "Be sure to stay on the paths. You have a watch, so be back by three."

I wasn't really looking forward to the hike. I would have rather challenged Kwan to a video game car race. He was so excited to be here, though. I felt like I had to humor him. He would see just how boring it was, and then we could stay in tomorrow.

Again, everything Kwan saw amazed him. Birds, trees, grass, everything made him yell and point. I was wondering if something was wrong with him.

Finally, he got my attention when we were walking through the field. All of a sudden, we saw a throng of hawks circling over one particular area. We sat down to watch them. We both had binoculars, so we got a really good look at the birds. They certainly were mighty! Their claws looked like they could pick up a person.

All of a sudden, whoosh! A hawk swooped down and grabbed something. We couldn't see what it was. A peek through the binoculars showed us it was a mouse! How cool! We had just seen a predator in action! I had to agree that was more interesting than a video game car race.

We kept going on our excursion, and now we entered the woods. It was cool and damp. That was a relief after the hot sun beating down on us in the open field. We saw a fallen tree and decided to have a seat and a drink of water. Both of us plunked down on the log.

Then we heard some rustling and noticed some movement in the grass. Believe me, we were silent and still when we watched the skunks slowly walk away. Apparently, we were sitting on their house. I never knew they lived in hollowed out trees.

Finally, when they were out of spraying range, Kwan whispered, "Can you believe that? That was really awesome! I have never been that close to a wild animal!" Again, I had to admit that seeing those skunks was pretty cool and pretty scary at the same time.

Our trip through the woods got even better. Kwan pointed out a tree that was almost ready to topple because it had so many termites eating away at it. We also saw a beehive and used the binoculars to check it out!

We waded in the little stream that went through the woods and saw crayfish and tiny little fish. If I had brought a cup, I would have taken some home. We heard a hammering noise. Kwan said it reminded him of a jackhammer. It turned out to be a woodpecker. The list of all the great things we saw goes on and on. It was just the first day of his visit!

When we returned home, we were both exhausted. Before bed, Kwan and I talked about what we would do the next day and the next. It was a fantastic week. It was a week of discovery. I learned more about the farm and the country from a city boy than I could see with my own eyes. When I went back to school, I'd have a lot of interesting things to write about!

Think Critically

1. Which character undergoes a change in the story?

2. What effect does Kwan's visit have on Emilio?

3. How would you feel if you had to move to a new environment? Explain your answer.

4. Which season do you think this story takes place? Explain your reason.

5. What happens at the end of the story?

Social Studies

Dueling Descriptions If you and your family could live anywhere in the world, where would you live? Find out about that place and then write a paragraph or two about how it would be different from the place you live now.

School-Home Connection Tell a family member about the story. Talk about times when looking at something from another person's point of view might be important.